This book belongs to

....

Fun Ideas for the Storyteller

Don't Rock the Boat! is an amusing story about a bunch of funny animals. It will make children laugh – and also encourage them to count. Children will love looking at the pictures, joining in with the text, and guessing what will happen at the end.

Read on to find out how to get the most fun out of this story.

Read and count

This story combines reading, counting, and fun. Read it right through first so that your child will enjoy the joke. As you read it for a second time, encourage your child to count the animals with you. At the end of the story, you could also count the presents and the animals' party hats.

3 puppies

Animal talk

At the end of the story, Dottie the Donkey says, *"Hee-haw! Hee-haw!"* Point to the other animals in the story and talk to your child about the noises they might make. Ask him which of the animal noises he likes best. Your child will enjoy making the noises with you as you read the story.

Hee-haw! Hee-haw!

Oink! Oink!

Hee-haw!

Oink! Oink!

Don't rock the boat!

Enjoy the repetition

There are lots of repeated phrases that give this story a rhythm and pattern that your child will soon remember. Once you have read the story a few times, your child will love joining in. Let her call out, *"Can we come with you?"*, wait for her to name the animals that come next, and encourage her to shout out, *"Don't rock the boat!"*

Saying the repeated phrases, following the words, and turning the pages will increase your child's enjoyment of the story and make her more confident about reading.

Story clues

Looking at the pictures and predicting what will happen is an important skill when learning to read. Before you, or your child, turn the page, look at the pictures and ask your child if he thinks the animals are going to rock the boat. Can he guess what might happen if the animals do rock the boat?

Have a good time counting and enjoy the story!

Wendy Cooling

Wendy Cooling
Reading Consultant

For my father, Peter W. Battle – Sarah Battle

DK

LONDON, NEW YORK, SYDNEY, DELHI, PARIS,
MUNICH and JOHANNESBURG

First published in Great Britain in 2001
by Dorling Kindersley Limited,
80 Strand, London WC2R 0RL

2 4 6 8 10 9 7 5 3 1

A CIP catalogue record for this book is available from the British Library.

ISBN 0-7513-2804-9

Colour reproduction by Dot Gradations, UK
Printed in Hong Kong by Wing King Tong

Acknowledgements:
Series Reading Consultant: Wendy Cooling   **Activities Adviser:** Dawn Sirett
Photographer: Zara Ronchi   **Models:** Hannah Shone, Cal Stuart and Juliett Preston

see our complete
catalogue at
www.dk.com

Don't Rock the Boat!

Sally Grindley

Illustrated by Sarah Battle

A Pearson Company

"What a glorious day for Dottie the Donkey's birthday party!" said Charlie the Cat.
"I'll go there in my boat, but I'll have to be careful not to get wet."

"Can I come with you?" came a voice from the shore.

One fluffy duckling was flapping up and down.

"You can come with me," said Charlie the Cat,
"but whatever you do, **don't rock the boat!**"

The fluffy duckling climbed in oh, so carefully,
and she didn't rock the boat, not a jiggle not a jot.

"Can we come with you?" came voices from the shore. Two happy hens were scooting round and round.

"You can come, too," said Charlie the Cat,
"but whatever you do, **don't rock the boat!**"

The two happy hens climbed in oh, so carefully,
and they only rocked the boat just a jiggle and a jot.

"Can we come with you?"
came voices from the shore.
Three playful puppies were
chasing each other's tails.

"You can come, too," said Charlie the Cat,
"but whatever you do, **don't rock the boat!**"

The three playful puppies
climbed in rather carelessly and
rocked the boat with a jostle and a jog.

"Can we come with you?"
came voices from the shore.
Four frisky lambs were
leaping up and down.

"You can come, too," said Charlie the Cat,
"but whatever you do, **don't rock the boat!**"

The four frisky lambs climbed in
very carelessly and rocked the boat
with a joggle and a jolt.

"Can we come with you?" came voices from the shore.
Five plump piglets were racing round and round.

"You can come, too," said Charlie the Cat,
"but whatever you do, **don't rock the boat!**"

The five plump piglets jumped in oh, so wildly,
that they rocked the boat.
Oh, yes they did! They rocked the boat and ...

...over it went!

"I said, 'Don't rock the boat!'"
cried Charlie the Cat.

At last they reached the party with a splish, splash, splosh, and how Dottie the Donkey laughed.

Can you find one duckling, two hens,
three puppies, four lambs, and five piglets?

Hee-haw! Hee-haw!

Activities to Enjoy

I f you've enjoyed this story, you might
like to try some of these simple, fun
activities with your child.

Sink the boat

In the story, the animals overturn their
boat. Ask your child to try to sink a toy
bath boat. See how many things you need
to put into the boat before it sinks. If you
don't have a toy boat, you could use an
empty plastic container. Ask your child to
splash the water to rock the boat and see
if that makes the boat turn over and sink.

Number frieze

Help your child to make a number frieze for the
numbers one to five using the animals from the story.
Divide a strip of paper into five sections. Ask your
child to draw one duckling on the first section, two
hens on the next section, three puppies on the next,
etc. Then write the correct number on each drawing.
Hang up the frieze when it is finished. You could also
sing number rhymes to familiarize your child with
the numbers one to five. Try *Five Little Speckled Frogs*
or *Five Little Monkeys Jumping on the Bed*.

Have a party!

Suggest having a pretend birthday party for one of your child's toys. Help her to make party hats. Make cone hats or crowns like the ones in the story. Stick on glitter, tassels, and coloured paper shapes to decorate the hats. You could also lay out some food for the party or make pretend food out of empty packets.

Invitations and presents

Ask your child to choose toys to come to the party. Help her to make invitations for the guests. You could also wrap empty packets to make presents. When the party is ready, don't forget to sing *Happy Birthday!*

Dear James
Please come
to my party
on..................
at..................

Other Share-a-Story titles to collect:

Lemono P by Sam McBratney,
illustrated by Catharine O'Neill

You're a Big Bear now, Winston Brown! by Paul May,
illustrated by Selina Young

Clara and Buster Go Moondancing by Dyan Sheldon,
illustrated by Caroline Anstey

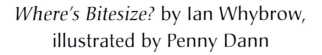

Where's Bitesize? by Ian Whybrow,
illustrated by Penny Dann

Mama Tiger, Baba Tiger by Juli Mahr,
illustrated by Graham Percy

I Like Me by Laurence Anholt,
illustrated by Adriano Gon

Nigel's Numberless World by Lucy Coats,
illustrated by Neal Layton

Not Now, Mrs Wolf! by Shen Roddie,
illustrated by Selina Young

The Caterpillar That Roared by Michael Lawrence,
illustrated by Alison Bartlett

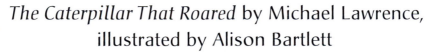

Are You Spring? by Caroline Pitcher,
illustrated by Cliff Wright